This edition published by Parragon Books Ltd in 2017

Parragon Books Ltd
Chartist House
15–17 Trim Street
Bath BA1 1HA, UK
www.parragon.com

ISBN 978-1-4748-9870-6

Printed in China

Disney PRINCESS

Tangled

PaRRagon

Bath • New York • Cologne • Melbourne • Delhi
Hong Kong • Shenzhen • Singapore

Once upon a time, in a land far away, a single drop of sunlight fell to the ground. It grew into a magical golden flower which possessed healing powers.

A vain, selfish old woman named Mother Gothel found the flower, and learned to unlock its abilities. For many centuries she kept the blossom a secret, using its magic to keep herself young and beautiful.

One day, the queen of the kingdom fell seriously ill. Desperate for a cure, the townspeople eventually found the legendary flower. Mother Gothel watched in horror as they uprooted it and carried it away.

The queen drank a potion made from the flower's blossom and instantly recovered. Soon after, she gave birth to a beautiful baby girl.

Furious at losing the flower, Mother Gothel crept into the nursery late one night. When she discovered that the flower's magic lived on in the baby's hair, she snatched the child away.

The king and queen were heartbroken. Every year afterwards, on their daughter's birthday, the grieving couple released lanterns into the night sky.

Mother Gothel raised the princess, Rapunzel, inside a soaring tower in a hidden valley.

"The outside world is a dangerous place," Mother Gothel often said. She wanted to make sure that Rapunzel – and her magical hair – stayed under her control.

But being confined never dampened Rapunzel's spirit. She and her chameleon friend, Pascal, had lots of interests like music and painting.

"Rapunzel! Let down your hair!" Mother Gothel called one afternoon, just as she always did whenever she arrived home to the tower.

As usual, Rapunzel pulled Mother Gothel up.

Today was different, though. It was the day before Rapunzel's eighteenth birthday, and she had a special request.

"I want to travel to see the floating lights!" she said. "They appear every year on my birthday – only on my birthday. I have to know what they are."

"Oh, you mean the stars," Mother Gothel quickly lied. She insisted that the outside world was too scary for a helpless girl like Rapunzel. "Don't ever ask to leave this tower again," she said.

Meanwhile, in another part of the forest, a thief named Flynn Rider came to an abrupt halt. He was travelling with the Stabbington brothers, and they were all on the run for theft from the palace ... but couldn't the WANTED poster have made him look just a little more handsome?

Just then, Flynn saw the palace guards on horseback close behind them. He grabbed the satchel containing the stolen goods and ran, leaving the Stabbington brothers behind.

The palace guards on their horses galloped hard after Flynn. The Captain of the Guard fell from his saddle during the chase, and Flynn hopped on to it. But Maximus, the palace horse, knew exactly what was happening. He fought furiously for the satchel.

Maximus bucked, and the satchel
flew onto a tree branch over a cliff's edge.
Flynn reached the bag first. "Ha ha!" he said.
 CRACK!
 The tree branch splintered, and both
of them toppled into the canyon below.

After they crash-landed, Flynn grabbed the bag and escaped into the bushes. As he felt his way along a rock face, he was surprised to discover an opening to a tunnel hidden behind a curtain of leaves.

Scrambling along it, he soon halted in astonishment. There, in the centre of a hidden valley, stood an enormous tower. It was the perfect hiding place.

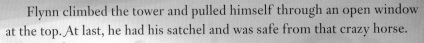

Flynn climbed the tower and pulled himself through an open window at the top. At last, he had his satchel and was safe from that crazy horse.

CLANG!

Rapunzel had hit Flynn with her frying pan. He was out cold!

Thinking quickly, she stuffed him into a wardrobe and propped a chair against the door. Rapunzel felt pleased with herself. Surely this act of bravery would prove to Mother Gothel that she could handle herself.

Noticing Flynn's satchel, Rapunzel reached inside and pulled out a sparkling gold crown! Something about it seemed familiar....

"Oh, Rapunzel! Let down your hair!" Mother Gothel called, interrupting Rapunzel's thoughts.

Rapunzel hid the crown before pulling Mother Gothel up, hoping to impress with her story of the intruder.

But Mother Gothel wouldn't listen. "You are not leaving this tower! EVER!" she screamed.

Rapunzel was shocked. Realizing she would never be allowed to leave the tower, she asked for a special paint for her birthday instead. It was three days' travel away.

Relieved, Mother Gothel agreed to fetch it for her.

After Mother Gothel left, Rapunzel pulled
Flynn out of the wardrobe.

She tied him to a chair with her hair, and when
he woke she explained her plan. "Tomorrow, these
lights will appear in the night sky. You will take me
to see them, and return me home safely. Then, and
only then, will I return your satchel to you."

Flynn was forced to agree.

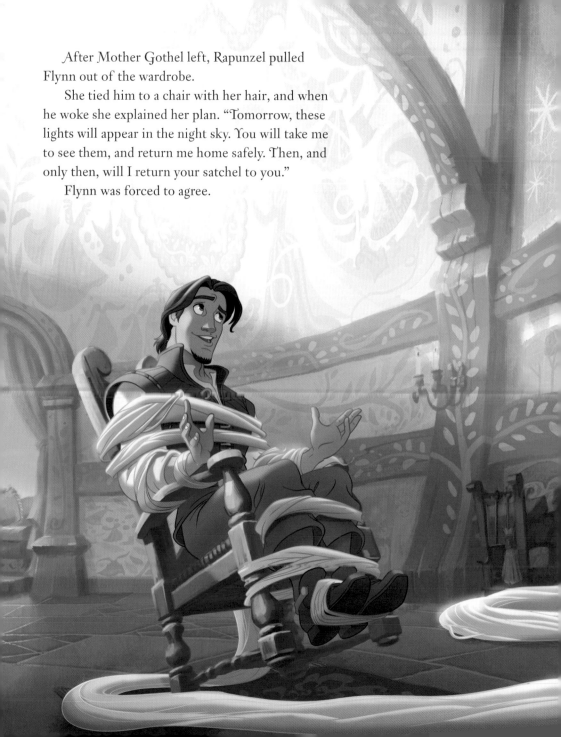

Rapunzel slid down the tower on her hair, and slowly touched one foot to the soft grass. "Woo-hoo!" she said. Her adventure had begun.

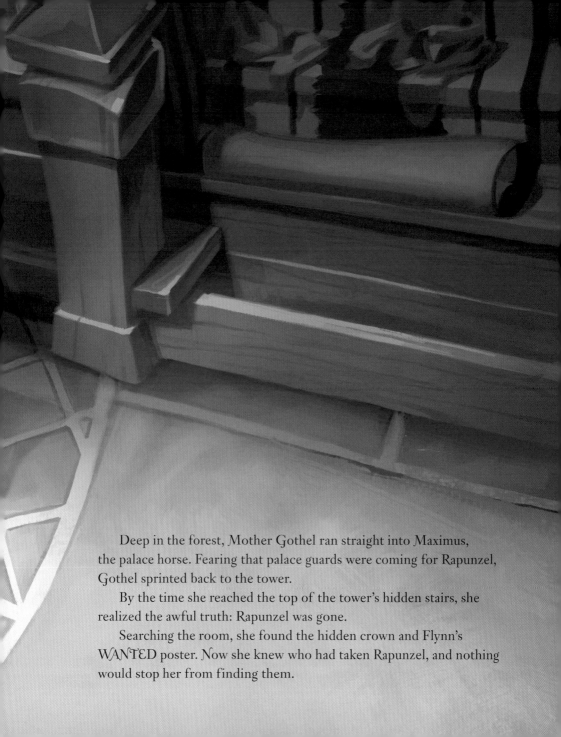

Deep in the forest, Mother Gothel ran straight into Maximus,
the palace horse. Fearing that palace guards were coming for Rapunzel,
Gothel sprinted back to the tower.

By the time she reached the top of the tower's hidden stairs, she
realized the awful truth: Rapunzel was gone.

Searching the room, she found the hidden crown and Flynn's
WANTED poster. Now she knew who had taken Rapunzel, and nothing
would stop her from finding them.

Trying to frighten Rapunzel into going home, Flynn took her to a pub called the Snuggly Duckling. The place was filled with scary men, one of Rapunzel's worst fears!

But it wasn't long before the thugs recognized Flynn from a WANTED poster. They grabbed him and started fighting over the reward money.

Rapunzel climbed on to a table. "Put him down!" she said, explaining that she needed Flynn to take her to see the lights. "Haven't any of you ever had a dream?"

In fact, every one of the thugs had a dream, and they each told Rapunzel what it was. No one noticed Mother Gothel creep to the window and peer inside....

Suddenly, palace guards burst into the pub.
They were followed by Maximus and the
Stabbingtons – who were now in shackles.
"Where's Rider?" asked the captain.
The pub thugs had grown fond of Rapunzel, and had
already helped her and Flynn escape into a hidden tunnel.
But Maximus soon sniffed out the secret passageway.
Horse and guards charged into the tunnel, continuing the chase.

The guards soon caught up with Flynn and Rapunzel
as they raced down the tunnel, and skidded to a stop at
the edge of an enormous cavern.

Just as Maximus closed in on Flynn, Rapunzel threw
him her hair. Flynn leaped from the cliff and swung
down, grabbing Rapunzel on the way.

When Flynn and Rapunzel landed at the bottom of the cavern, they realized the Stabbingtons were right behind them. The brothers had escaped from the guards and wanted to take the stolen crown back.

Suddenly, the dam above them burst. A giant wave of water swept through the cavern, washing the thugs away along with Maximus and the guards. Flynn and Rapunzel ducked into a cave just in time!

The cave entrance collapsed behind them, and water began to pour in. Flynn tried to find a way to escape the rising water, but it was dark and he cut his hand.

"I'm so sorry, Flynn," said Rapunzel.

"Eugene. My real name's Eugene Fitzherbert," said Flynn.

Since they were telling secrets, Rapunzel whispered, "I have magic hair that glows when I sing."

Suddenly, Rapunzel realized her hair might save
them! She began singing the special song that woke the
magic, and then she dived underwater. The glow from her
hair revealed a hole in the rocks – an escape route!

Free at last, Rapunzel and Flynn dragged themselves to dry land.
"Your hair glows," Flynn said in disbelief. "Why?"

"It doesn't just glow," Rapunzel said. Again she sang, and her hair healed Flynn's hand. She explained about her hair's magic and told him about Mother Gothel ... and the tower.

Finally, Flynn began to understand.

Mother Gothel had tracked Rapunzel down, and waited
in the shadows for her to be alone. Now she knew Rapunzel
hadn't been kidnapped, she had come up with a new plan –
with the Stabbington brothers.

Mother Gothel gave Rapunzel the satchel, and dared her
to see if Flynn would stick around once he had the crown back.

The next morning, Flynn woke with a start. Maximus had found him!

The horse grabbed Flynn's boot and started to drag him away. Luckily, Rapunzel was able to coax Maximus into letting go. Then she stroked his neck. "He's nothing but a big sweetheart," she said fondly.

Rapunzel insisted that Maximus and Flynn cooperate, just for one day. After all, she wanted to see the lights. "And did I mention it's my birthday?" she added.

Finally, Maximus and Flynn agreed. They followed the sound of bells, which would lead them to the kingdom.

Together with Flynn, Pascal and Maximus, Rapunzel stepped through the gates and into the bustle of the town. It was so exciting!

Flynn bought a flag with the kingdom's emblem – a golden sun – and gave it to Rapunzel. Then some little girls excitedly offered to braid Rapunzel's hair.

Rapunzel's attention was caught by a mosaic on a wall.
It showed the king and queen holding a baby girl with green
eyes – just like her own. She learned that the lanterns were
intended to honour this lost princess.

Music filled the square, and Rapunzel and Flynn
joined hands to dance with the crowd.
They were carried away by the music, the dance and
the pure happiness they felt at just being together.

As evening fell, Flynn led Rapunzel
to a boat and rowed into the harbour,
providing a perfect view of the kingdom.

Lanterns began to fill the sky, and
Rapunzel's heart soared. Then Flynn
handed Rapunzel her own lantern.

In return, Rapunzel offered Flynn
the satchel she'd kept hidden all day.
She felt confident now, no longer
afraid that he would leave her
when he had the crown.

Just then, Flynn spotted the Stabbington brothers on shore.
He quickly rowed the boat to land.

"I'll be right back," he told Rapunzel.

Flynn was done with being a thief, so he tossed the satchel to
the brothers. But they didn't care. Mother Gothel had told them
about Rapunzel's magical hair, and they wanted her instead.

Before Flynn could react, the brothers knocked him unconscious.
They tied him up in a boat and sent him sailing into the harbour.

Rapunzel waited, but Flynn did not return. Instead, the Stabbington brothers emerged from the shadows. They lied, saying that Flynn had traded her for the crown.

Rapunzel was heartbroken. She ran from the Stabbingtons – then heard a scuffle behind her, and Mother Gothel's voice. "Rapunzel?"

"Mother?" Rapunzel found Mother Gothel standing over the brothers. She'd knocked them out, to 'save' Rapunzel.

"You were right, Mother," Rapunzel said. She was ready to go home.

When Flynn's boat bumped against the pier,
the palace guards immediately saw the stolen crown.
They didn't care that Flynn's hands had been tied
to the ship's wheel. They threw him into prison.
But Maximus was watching from nearby.
He understood that Flynn had been set up – and that
Rapunzel was in danger. Somehow, he had to help!

Inside the prison, Flynn saw the Stabbingtons had
been locked in their own cell. Mother Gothel had double-
crossed them, and they were furious.

Suddenly, the pub thugs arrived! Maximus had fetched
them to help break Flynn out of prison. Working together,
the thugs launched Flynn over the prison wall, right on to
Maximus's back.

Now it was time to rescue Rapunzel.

Back in the tower, Rapunzel looked at the golden
sun symbol on the kingdom flag. Then she gazed at her
paintings on the ceiling ... she had been painting that
same symbol her entire life!

Suddenly, she realized the shocking truth.

"I am the lost princess," Rapunzel told Mother Gothel, grabbing her arm. "And I will never let you use my hair again."

Gothel yanked her arm away, falling backwards into a mirror that shattered against the floor.

Flynn and Maximus raced through the forest. They knew Rapunzel was in danger, and they needed to reach her quickly.

At the tower, Flynn leaped off Maximus's back. "Rapunzel? Rapunzel, let down your hair!" he called.

Golden hair cascaded to the ground. Relieved, Flynn began to climb.

"Rapunzel, I thought I'd never see you again," he said as he stepped through the window. But it wasn't Rapunzel who was waiting for him.

It was Mother Gothel – and she stabbed Flynn!
Poor Rapunzel, tied with chains, watched in horror.

As Flynn collapsed, Mother Gothel dragged
Rapunzel to the trapdoor. But Rapunzel fought with
all her strength.

"I will never stop trying to get away from you!"
she cried. "But if you let me save him, I will go
with you. I promise."

Mother Gothel agreed. She knew Rapunzel
never broke a promise.

Rapunzel rushed to Flynn's side and placed
her hair over his wound.

"I can't let you do this," Flynn said.
He would rather die than allow Rapunzel
to be imprisoned forever.

Flynn touched Rapunzel's cheek. Then he
grabbed a shard from the broken mirror ... and
cut off her hair! Instantly, it turned brown
and lost its healing power.

"What have you done?" Mother Gothel shrieked. She stared into the broken mirror, watching as her image grew older and older. Within moments, she aged hundreds of years and turned to dust.

Flynn closed his eyes and his head fell back. He was gone.

Rapunzel began to cry ... and a single golden tear fell on Flynn's cheek. Suddenly, the tear began to glow, spreading across Flynn's body, healing him.

His eyes fluttered open again. Rapunzel wrapped her arms round him, and the two of them shared their first kiss.

Flynn and Maximus took Rapunzel straight to the castle. The king and queen knew immediately who she was, and rushed to embrace her. They were overcome with joy that their daughter had finally returned.

Rapunzel felt her parents' love surround her as they all held tightly to one another, a family together at last.

The entire kingdom celebrated
Princess Rapunzel's return. Hundreds of
glowing lanterns were once again launched
into the sky. Their light had finally guided
Rapunzel home.

Rapunzel's and Flynn's dreams came true,
along with those of their friends and family.
They found everlasting love ... and lived
happily ever after.